A Garden Grows

by Rachel Kranz
illustrated by Leslie Bowman

Chapters

Harcourt

Orlando   Boston   Dallas   Chicago   San Diego

Visit *The Learning Site!*

www.harcourtschool.com

Getting Started

Todd looked at his father eagerly. "Ms. Jameson said I could borrow her tools. She has a rake and a hoe and everything."

Todd's father knew what he was talking about. Todd wanted to have a garden. His family had never lived in a place with a backyard, so he had never had a garden of his own.

Now Todd had a chance to have his own little garden, and he didn't want to let it go by. He finally stopped talking to let his father have a word.

"All right," his father said, recognizing Todd's determination. "You can try it, as long as it's something you really want."

Todd's neighbor, Ms. Jameson, had told him about the neighborhood's community garden, right down the block. The garden was really a huge vacant lot divided into squares. If you lived in the community, you could get permission to grow flowers and vegetables in your own little plot.

Todd slid the application form across the kitchen table so his father could look at it.

"See, Dad?" he said. "We just have to fill out this application form."

Todd's father nodded and helped him fill it out. They read each line and filled in the information. Todd printed as neatly and carefully as he could.

Name _TODD MILLER_
Address _____
_____
Telephone _____
How long have you lived at your current address?
_____

Todd watched patiently as his father signed the form. Then a smile burst across his face.

"You're really excited about this," Todd's father said.

"Yes," Todd answered, "It will be amazing to have a place to grow things. I think I'll be good at it, too," he added.

"I can understand how you feel," his father said. "When I retire from working, I want to live where it's warm so I can have a garden all year long. It is something I have been thinking about for a long time."

Have you ever had a community garden plot before?
no
If you are under 18, you must have the signature of a parent or guardian:

Arvin L. Miller

"Just remember," Todd's father said, "caring for a garden is a lot of work. A garden requires constant attention."

"I know," Todd said eagerly, "but I can handle it. Ms. Jameson is going to help me. She said she'd show me everything I need to know."

"I was wondering if I could take this form over to Ms. Jameson now," Todd continued. "She said she'd turn it in for me."

"Sure," said Mr. Miller, "I'll walk over with you so I can thank Ms. Jameson for encouraging you to do this."

Ms. Jameson invited them in. "Not everybody gets a plot," she explained. "Sometimes there aren't enough spaces for everyone. If that happens, you'll just have to wait until next year." She looked at Todd's anxious face. "I have a good feeling about this," she added, "so don't worry."

Days passed, and Todd waited eagerly to hear whether he would be getting a garden plot. Sure enough, a few days later, a large white envelope from the Community Garden Board arrived.

Todd held his breath as he opened the envelope and took out the letter.

Dear Todd Miller:

We are happy to inform you that your application for a community garden plot has been approved. Here is a map showing you where your garden is. Good luck, and happy gardening!

Sincerely,

Margarita Lopez

Margarita Lopez, President
Community Garden Board.

You have been assigned plot #E-5

	A	B	C	D	E	F	G	H
1								
2								
3								
4								
5					▓			
6								
7								

The next day, Todd and Ms. Jameson went to the garden. Todd read the sign above the entrance. It reminded gardeners to respect their neighbors, and Todd made a silent promise that he would.

"Come on," said Ms. Jameson, "let's go locate your plot." As they followed the map, they saw that people were already working in other plots along the way. Ms. Jameson and Todd finally found his exact plot.

"Here it is," Ms. Jameson said, "and it belongs to you, at least for this summer."

Todd looked at the plot and imagined vegetables growing there. On the other hand, perhaps he would rather grow flowers.

"Some of the other gardeners have already started," Todd said.

"Yes," Ms. Jameson said. "Many people have had gardens here before, and they come back year after year. They are sprucing up their plots after the long, hard winter."

Then she stopped for a minute and breathed in deeply. "Oh, I just adore the fresh smell of garden soil," she said.

"Me, too," thought Todd, breathing deeply. He was very happy now that his gardening adventure was finally about to begin!

How Does Your Garden Grow?

Todd soon realized that he had never worked so hard in his life! Ms. Jameson had lent him some of her gardening tools and showed him how to break up the hard soil.

"You really need to shake things up," she explained. "Lots of air needs to get mixed into that dirt so that your plants can breathe."

Todd felt as though he had been hoeing for hours, but every time he thought he had done enough, Ms. Jameson shook her head.

"Not yet," she said patiently. "Keep working, keep working."

Finally, Ms. Jameson told Todd he was ready to plant. "Now, where are your seeds?" she asked.

Todd's face fell, and he admitted that he didn't have any. "How could I have forgotten?" he asked himself.

"Well, that's all right," said Ms. Jameson, recognizing Todd's disappointment. "You can just run over to the store and get some."

Unfortunately, it was late Saturday afternoon and the neighborhood stores were closed. Todd was disappointed that his gardening adventure had to stop so soon. "What can I do?" he wondered.

Todd looked around at his neighbors, who were so busy planting. He was the only person just standing around.

Then he noticed an enormous bag of birdseed lying on the ground. It didn't seem to belong to anyone. "What would happen if I planted the birdseed?" he wondered. "What would grow?" Very curious, he picked up the sack of birdseed. "I'll plant this," he announced.

"Birdseed?" said Ms. Jameson. "What do you plan to grow, birds?"

They both laughed. "Maybe planting birdseed is not a bad idea," she said. "Give it a try."

So Todd planted his birdseed garden. Word spread quickly among the other gardeners. As time passed, they began asking about his garden—and teasing him.

"Hey, Todd!" Mr. Zowicki said on the way to his own plot of carrots and cabbages. "What are you growing there, birds?"

"We'll see," said Todd, as he spread compost on his little garden.

"Well, Todd," said Angela Gomez, as she weeded her lilies and hollyhocks, "I've always liked birds. Hope you'll save me a lark or two!"

"We'll see," Todd said again, as he carefully weeded and watered his crop.

Growing Birds

Days passed, and Todd's birdseed garden quickly began to sprout and grow. Millet grew from the millet seed, and beautiful yellow sunflowers began to blossom from the sunflower seeds. Nothing grew from the cracked corn or the thistle.

"What good will those plants do you?" asked Mr. Zowicki. "Carrots and cabbages make good soup, but you can't do much with your crop!"

"Wait and see," said Todd.

"Lilies and hollyhocks are beautiful to look at," said Angela Gomez, "and so are your sunflowers, but what good is that other stuff?"

"Wait and see," said Todd.

End of Summer Picnic!
Bring food and flowers
from Your Garden to
Share with Your Neighbors!

Then one day, a blue jay flew into Todd's garden
and landed on a millet plant.

"See," Todd said proudly, "I *am* growing birds!"

A bright red cardinal followed the blue jay. It
started to eat the sunflower seeds.

"Would you rather have a red bird or a blue jay?"
Todd asked Angela. "I have both!"

The next day, the brightly colored birds were
joined by two grosbeaks, a grackle, and a goldfinch.
The day after that, along came a dove and two
chickadees. Pretty soon, Todd's garden was filled
with all kinds of beautiful birds.

Everyone who passed had to smile.

On the day of the end-of-summer picnic, the gardeners brought things to share. Some brought food they had grown, and some shared flowers from their gardens.

Todd was disappointed that he hadn't anything to share.

"Don't worry," Mr. Zowicki said. "You've been sharing with us all along."

"Have I?" Todd asked.

"Well, look," Mr. Zowicki said, pointing to two red cardinals that had come to the picnic. "You shared your birds every day and we loved them!"

Todd smiled at that thought. "Now what do you think I should grow next year?"